Dear Parent:
Your child's love of reading starts here!

Every child learns to read in a different way and at his or her own speed. Some go back and forth between reading levels and read favorite books again and again. Others read through each level in order. You can help your young reader improve and become more confident by encouraging his or her own interests and abilities. From books your child reads with you to the first books he or she reads alone, there are I Can Read Books for every stage of reading:

SHARED READING
Basic language, word repetition, and whimsical illustrations, ideal for sharing with your emergent reader

BEGINNING READING
Short sentences, familiar words, and simple concepts for children eager to read on their own

READING WITH HELP
Engaging stories, longer sentences, and language play for developing readers

READING ALONE
Complex plots, challenging vocabulary, and high-interest topics for the independent reader

ADVANCED READING
Short paragraphs, chapters, and exciting themes for the perfect bridge to chapter books

I Can Read Books have introduced children to the joy of reading since 1957. Featuring award-winning authors and illustrators and a fabulous cast of beloved characters, I Can Read Books set the standard for beginning readers.

A lifetime of discovery begins with the magical words "I Can Read!"

Visit www.icanread.com for information
on enriching your child's reading experience.

For Ella,
Enjoy!
—R.S.

I Can Read Book® is a trademark of HarperCollins Publishers.

Library of Congress Cataloging-in-Publication Data is available.
ISBN 978-0-06-197860-9 (trade bdg.) —ISBN 978-0-06-197859-3 (pbk.)

12 13 14 15 16 SCP   10 9 8 7 6 5 4 3 2 1   ❖   First Edition

I Can Read!™

BEGINNING 1 READING

Splat the Cat
Takes the Cake

Based on the bestselling books by Rob Scotton

Cover art by Rob Scotton

Text by Amy Hsu Lin

Interior illustrations by Robert Eberz

HARPER

An Imprint of HarperCollins*Publishers*

Splat the cat

sat watching *Super Cat* on TV.

It was his favorite show.

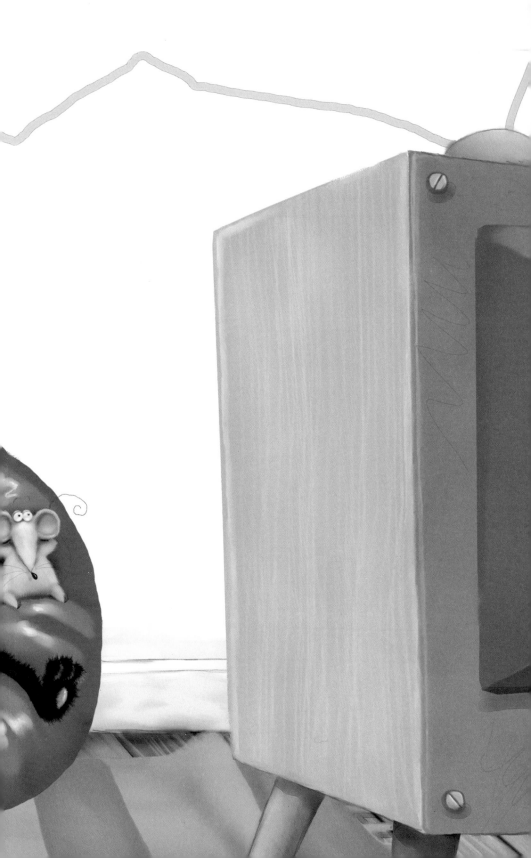

This time, brave Super Cat
was saving his tiny town
from an awful earthquake!

Splat said, "I want to be
a brave hero, too.
Eek! Look out—a snake!
Seymour, I'll save you!"

So Splat saved Seymour

from a sneaky snake.

8

But he forgot to beware
of his mango milkshake . . .

SPLAT!

"That's that!" exclaimed Dad.
"No more Super Cat.
No more TV."

"No more TV?" Splat groaned.

"No more TV!" said his mom.

"Why not take a bike ride to the lake?"

"Yes, I could use a break," said Splat.

Splat took off on his bike.

Riding helped him shake

his mango milkshake mistake.

On his way to the lake,

Splat saw a big sign.

A clever thought crossed his mind.

He could bake a TV-winning cake.

Splat never made it to the lake.

Instead, he sped home

to bake his cake.

He opened Mom's cake book

and looked and flipped.

But no cake in that book

had the tippy-top look

of a super first-prize cake.

So Splat said, "I'll bake

my own super-duper cake.

One that nobody else can make!"

Splat said, "Let's see.

I'll need a large pan or two,

or maybe three."

Splat put in

all the things he needed

to bake a super-duper cake.

Splat said to Seymour,

"More cake flour

makes more cake power!"

Then he added one more thing.

The cake was now ready to bake.

But that last thing Splat added

was a big, BIG mistake!

SPLAT!

Now there was no cake.

And there was a BIG mess.

Splat was too tired to bake
another cake.
He went to bed thinking,
"How will I win the TV?
What would Super Cat do?"

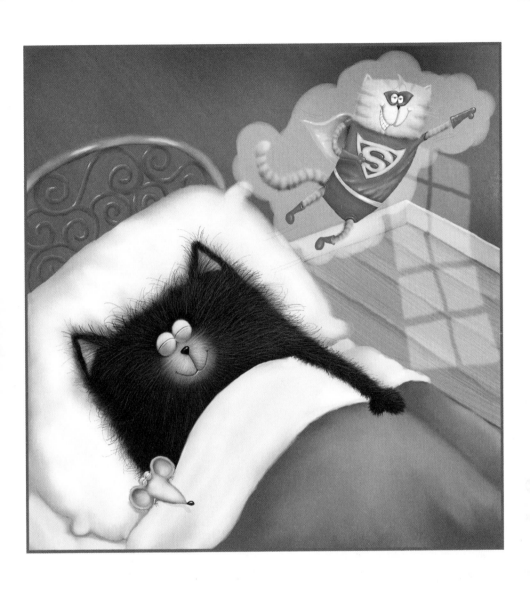

Then Splat dreamed

of Super Cat.

When Splat woke up

he knew what to do

and how to bake his super cake.

At the contest, Splat was ready.

Spike was there with his cake.

Kitten was there with her cake.

Plank had baked a cake, too.

Spike's cake was wider.

Kitten's cake was prettier.

Plank's cake was taller.

Was Splat's cake super enough?

The judges looked closely
at every cake baked.
They tasted the cakes.
They talked together.

Then one judge said,

"Our top judge will now

award the Super Cake prize."

Surprise!

The top judge was really Super Cat!

"Splat the cat takes the cake!"
said Super Cat.

"I mean he takes the TV."

Splat was very happy.

When he got home

he said, "Now it's time

to watch *Super Cat*!"

"It's you who takes the cake,
Super Cat," whispered Splat.